FRANKIE'S MAGIC FOOTBALL

GAME OVER!

FRANK LAMPARD

LITTLE, BROWN BOOKS FOR YOUNG READERS
www.lbkids.co.uk

LITTLE, BROWN BOOKS FOR YOUNG READERS

First published in Great Britain in 2018 by Hodder and Stoughton

13 5 7 9 10 8 6 4 2

A CIP catalogue record for this book
is available from the British Library.

ISBN 978-1-51020-185-9

Typeset in Cantarell by M Rules
Printed and bound in Great Britain by
Clays Ltd, St Ives plc

The paper and board used in this book are made
from wood from responsible sources.

Little, Brown Books for Young Readers
An imprint of
Hachette Children's Group
Part of Hodder and Stoughton
Carmelite House
50 Victoria Embankment
London EC4Y 0DZ

An Hachette UK Company
www.hachette.co.uk

www.hachettechildrens.co.uk

*To my mum Pat, who encouraged me
to do my homework in between kicking
a ball all around the house, and is still
with me every step of the way.*

*Welcome to a fantastic
Fantasy League – the greatest
football competition ever held
in this world or any other!*

*You'll need four on a team,
so choose carefully. This is a lot
more serious than a game in the
park. You'll never know who your
next opponents will be, or
where you'll face them.*

*So lace up your boots, players,
and good luck! The whistle's
about to blow!*

The Ref

CHAPTER 1

"Hop up on the bed here," said the doctor, peering over the top of his glasses.

Frankie lay on the examination table.

"So, what exactly happened?" asked the doctor.

"I was playing football," Frankie began, "and my foot caught the ground funny."

"It looks swollen," said Frankie's mum.

"It looks *smelly*," said Kevin. He was standing by the door of the doctor's office, and waved a hand in front of his face.

"Can you wiggle your toes?" asked the doctor, ignoring Frankie's brother.

Frankie did so, without any pain. His mum was right – the right side of his ankle did look bigger than normal.

The doctor took hold of Frankie's right foot in one hand, and his ankle in the other. "Tell me if you feel any discomfort."

Frankie lay back and let the
doctor rotate his foot. It was fine
at first, but as the doctor pushed
his toes to the left, hot pain shot
up his leg.

"Ouch!" he cried.

"Looks like you've just pulled a
few ligaments," said the doctor.

Frankie sat up on his elbows.
"So, it'll be okay?"

"A couple of weeks' rest should heal things up nicely," said the doctor.

Frankie stared at him in horror. "A couple of weeks! The town under-12 five-a-side tournament is happening in six days' time."

The doctor shrugged. "I'm sorry, Frankie – I can't see you recovering by then."

"But ..."

Frankie's mum patted his arm. "It's only a game, Frankie. I'm sure your team can find a replacement."

Disappointment sat like a heavy rock in Frankie's stomach.

4

They'd been working towards the tournament for weeks. Thirty-two teams, from all the different schools in town. He felt like he was letting everyone down – Charlie, Louise, Kobi and Hannah.

The doctor brought him a set of crutches. "These should be the right size. Come back early next week and we'll have another look at you. But don't get your hopes up about playing soon. You risk making the injury worse."

"Thank you," mumbled Frankie.

At home later that day, Frankie lay on his bed tossing his battered football against the wall and catching it again. The crutches leant up against the wall. Only his brother and his closest friends knew the magic the football possessed – the ability to open doorways in amazing worlds.

It's just a shame it can't magic my leg better, thought Frankie.

His bedroom door opened a fraction and Max scampered in. He looked at the football, tail wagging. Frankie's dog loved a kickaround, any time of day.

"Sorry, boy – I'm out of action," said Frankie. He'd broken the bad news to his friends over the phone.

6

They'd been really nice about it, but Frankie could tell they were disappointed too.

The only person who had seemed pleased was Kevin. His team had more chance of winning the tournament now.

The doorbell rang below, and Frankie heard his mum answer it. "He's in his room," she said. "I hope you can cheer him up!"

Footsteps pounded up the stairs and a moment later Charlie and Louise came in. Charlie had a full rucksack on his back.

"How are you doing?" asked Louise. "Does it hurt?"

Frankie shook his head. "Not much. Have you found someone to take my place?"

Charlie looked very glum. "Not yet. Everyone's already in a team. It won't be the same without you anyway."

"I'm really sorry," Frankie said.

"Stop apologising!" said Louise. "Injuries are part of life."

Frankie was glad he had such good friends. "Hey, Charlie, what's in the bag?" he asked, trying to change the subject.

Charlie's face brightened, as he pulled out his games console and controllers. "We might not be

able to play proper football," he said, "so this is the next best thing: *FantasyScorer2*."

"Cool!" said Frankie. He'd heard about the new football game from other kids. You could play with your friends against all sorts of different teams – on lava pitches, in space, under the sea. There were hundreds of levels. It reminded him of some of the real, crazy adventures he and his friends had undergone with the magic football.

"Where can we plug it in?" asked Charlie.

"My brother has a TV in his room," said Frankie.

He grabbed his crutches and they went across the landing to Kevin's bedroom. A sign on the door read "Keep Out – Dangerous Animal Inside!"

Frankie knocked, and Kevin's scowling face appeared.

"What do you want?" he asked.

"Can we plug in Charlie's console, please?" asked Frankie.

"No," said Kevin. "I'm busy." He began to shut the door, but then stopped. His eyes rested on the game in Charlie's hand. "Is that *FantasyScorer2*?"

"Yep!" said Louise.

Kevin swung the door open wide

to reveal his messy bedroom. "Then come on in," he said. "I've been dying to try it!"

Frankie shared a quick glance with his friends. It wasn't quite what they'd had in mind, but Kevin couldn't cause too many problems just playing a computer game.

And with his foot injured, he didn't have a lot of options!

CHAPTER 2

As Charlie booted up the game,
Frankie tried to clear a space on
the floor where they could all sit.
Kevin's room looked like a tornado
had blown through it. Dad said
they had to clean their rooms once
a week, but Kevin's hadn't seen a
vacuum cleaner for at least a year.

"Don't touch my stuff!" said
Frankie's brother, as Frankie moved

a mould-covered plate onto a shelf. Louise grimaced.

Max was by the door, tail drooping, with the magic football in his mouth. *Poor thing,* thought Frankie. *Dogs can't play computer games!*

"It's ready!" said Charlie. "But before we start playing, we need to design our avatars."

"Our what?" asked Louise.

"It means the characters who we'll play in the game," said Kevin, rolling his eyes and grabbing a controller. "I'll go first."

Kevin created an avatar on screen that looked more like a bodybuilder than Frankie's actual brother.

Then, the rest of them took turns. It was really fun finding the body shapes and hairstyles that looked like themselves, and they were able to choose special skills to match how they played. Frankie chose "striking power" and "speed", while Louise selected "tackling skills" and "passing accuracy". Charlie of course wanted to play as a goalkeeper and selected "reflexes". They all laughed as he hesitated for ages over the colour of his avatar's goalie gloves.

In the game, there were all sorts of options. Shoot-outs, one-on-one challenges or multi-player. Frankie went up against a team of ghosts in a haunted house, Louise played a game with an exploding football, and Charlie saved shots from a cannon on board a pirate ship! When it was Kevin's turn, he took a long time setting up, and then managed to dribble the ball around an entire team of sharks and score into an underwater cave.

"This game's so easy!" he said.

Charlie squinted and pointed to a small icon on the screen. It showed the referee tied up in a coil of rope. "That's because you've set the *cheat mode*," he said.

A fierce flush rose up Kevin's
cheeks. "It was an accident. How do
we take it off?"

Charlie took the controller and
toggled through a few screens, then
handed it back. "Now let's see how
good you really are."

They were just getting ready

to start a multi-player game, when Frankie's dad called from downstairs. "Dinner time!"

"No!" said Frankie. "I was enjoying this!"

Kevin stood up, obviously relieved not to have to play again, and tossed the controller on his unmade bed. "Oh well, another time! Looks like Charlie and Louise have to go home."

"I'm sure they can stay for dinner," said Frankie. "We could play more afterwards."

"Uh ... sure," said Kevin, shrugging.

As they left the room, Frankie

passed Max on the landing and gave him a stroke. His dog dropped the ball at Frankie's feet.

"I told you – I'm not allowed to play for two weeks," said Frankie.

Max looked up with sad eyes and laid his head on his front paws.

Charlie and Louise did stay for dinner – sausages and mash, Frankie's favourite. Louise was vegetarian, though, so she just had the potato with grated cheese.

As they finished, Frankie called his dog to eat the leftovers. Normally he'd have expected to hear Max's paws thundering down the stairs, but he didn't come.

"Weird," said Frankie. "I've never known him turn down a sausage."

"Maybe he's designing his own avatar," said Louise, grinning.

"Shall we go and have another game then?" said Frankie.

"Sorry," said Kevin, looking at the table. "I've got homework to do."

Frankie's eyes goggled. "Since when do you do your homework?"

"Since he doesn't want to be embarrassed," muttered Louise.

"Well, I am shocked, but pleased," said Frankie's mum. "I think Charlie had better take his console home with him, then. Kevin, you can help with the dishes."

Kevin sulked, but began to tidy away the plates.

Frankie trailed after his friends back upstairs, holding the banister for support. He called Max again as he did, and found his dog standing beside Kevin's closed bedroom door, the hackles across his neck raised.

"What's wrong, boy?" Frankie said.

A *thump* came from the other side of the bedroom door, making them all jump. Someone was inside!

Frankie's throat went dry.

Another *thump*.

"Is it a burglar?" said Charlie, face pale.

"Should we phone the police?" said Louise.

"I'll get Mum!" said Frankie. He backed off towards the stairs, then Max turned around and spoke.

"Not sure that's a great idea, Frankie," he growled.

"Huh? You're talking!" said Frankie. "You only talk when the football works its magic and opens a doorway."

Max's ears drooped guiltily. "Yes, about that . . ."

Thump. Thump.

"Who's in there?" said Louise, putting her hand on the door.

"Wait," said Max. "Let me explain. I was just playing with the football in Kevin's room . . ."

"The *magic* football?" said Charlie.

Max nodded. "It hit the computer. There were a few sparks, then next minute *he* appears."

Thump.

Frankie didn't understand at all, but he knew they couldn't tell Mum if it had something to do with the magic football. He drew a deep breath, pushed down the door handle and went into Kevin's room.

Charlie gasped, and Louise gripped his arm. Frankie couldn't believe what he was seeing. Lying on the bed, tossing the magic football against the wall, was a boy in football kit, about his own age. No, *exactly* the same age. And he had the same brown hair and eyes. It was like looking in the mirror.

"Hi!" said the stranger. "I suppose you must be Frankie."

"And you are . . . ?" said Frankie, mouth gaping.

The boy hopped off the bed and

balanced the magic football on the arch of his foot, then kicked it neatly across the room. It landed in Kevin's wastepaper basket and the boy held out a hand.

"I suppose I'm Frankie too."

CHAPTER 3

Max took the boy's hand, which
felt oddly cold and waxy. In fact,
looking closely at the new arrival,
his skin had a strange smooth
sheen. And his hair was perfectly
styled, with not a single strand
out of place. The computer screen
displayed a message: "DO YOU
REALLY WANT TO EXIT THE
GAME?"

Frankie glanced at the magic football, remembering what Max had said.

"You're my avatar!" he said. "You've come from the *FantasyScorer2* game!"

The new boy nodded. "Cool, isn't it?"

Charlie reached out and poked the boy's face with a finger. "You're actually real!"

"Seems like it," said the boy, smiling widely. His teeth were whiter than white.

Max's ears twitched and he trotted to the door. "Kevin's coming!" he said.

"Quick! Hide!" said Frankie to the boy.

"What?" said the avatar.

Frankie grabbed the new boy by the shoulders and steered him towards the wardrobe, bustling him inside.

"Just be quiet!" he said. "Please!"

A moment after Frankie closed the door, Kevin burst into his room. Everyone straightened up, even Max.

"What's going on?" asked Kevin.

"Nothing!" they said together.

Kevin shook his head in bewilderment. "Just unplug your

console, Freckles. I need my room back."

Charlie shot Frankie a glance that said *What shall we do?*

Frankie couldn't think straight. If they took the computer out, did that mean they couldn't get the pretend Frankie back into the game?

"What are you waiting for?" said Kevin.

A small creak came from the wardrobe door, and Frankie made a show of leaning against it.

"Something's going on ..." said Kevin.

From behind the wardrobe door,

a voice whispered, "Press the EXIT button."

Kevin's eyes narrowed. "Did someone just say something?" The wardrobe door bumped a little. "Who's in there?" said Kevin, eyes alarmed.

"No one!" said Louise.

But Kevin was already striding across the mess-strewn floor. "If it's another one of your friends, sneaking about in my room ..."

He grabbed Frankie and pulled him away from the door. At the same time, Charlie jumped the other way and snatched the controller off the floor. Kevin flung open the

wardrobe as Charlie thumbed the EXIT button and the screen blanked out.

The inside of the wardrobe was perfectly normal apart from the smell of Kevin's sports kit. There was no sign of the boy.

That was close!

"Told you," said Louise.

Kevin closed the door, and turned to where Frankie and his friends were hurriedly putting the console back into Charlie's rucksack. "Shouldn't you get busy trying to find a replacement player for your team, anyway?" he said. He picked up the football from his bin and tossed it through the door. "I've seen a scarecrow in the fields – you could ask him. Ha!"

He was still chuckling at his own feeble joke as Frankie and his friends left the room.

Frankie spoke to his friends at the front door, keeping his voice low. "Do you think he's gone for good?" he asked.

"I don't know," said Louise. "I feel bad for him, trapped in the game."

"He's just an avatar," said Charlie. "It's no big deal. It's where he belongs."

Frankie yawned. What with the visit to the doctor, and the strange

events of the afternoon, he was
really tired. Tomorrow was Monday,
and he still hadn't done his own
homework. He wished his friends
good night, then went back inside.
Max waited at the bottom of the
stairs, tail wagging. He followed
Frankie into the kitchen, and wolfed
down the two sausages in less
than ten seconds. Frankie managed
to relax a little. The magic had
obviously worn off.

Frankie was brushing his teeth before
bed when the phone rang downstairs.
His dad answered, then came up. "For
you Frankie. It's Charlie."

Frankie felt a tingling down his spine. He knew it was trouble before Charlie even spoke.

"He's back!" said his friend.

"Who?" Frankie replied, even though he had a pretty good idea already. He went back to his room and closed the door.

"Who do you think? You. Him. E–Frankie. Whatever it's called. As soon as I booted up the game, there he was. He took the lead controller and ran off!"

Frankie gripped the phone tighter. "Where's he gone?"

"I have no idea! I switched off the game, but I don't know—"

Frankie heard a knocking at his
window, and spun around. And
there he was, perched on the
sloping roof outside. *E-Frankie.*

"He's here," Frankie said to
Charlie. "I'd better go."

He hung up, and went across to
his window, opening it. E-Frankie
jumped inside. His kit, like his skin

and hair, was perfectly clean and smooth. In his hand, he held the missing controller. "Hello again," he said cheerfully.

"What are you doing here?" said Frankie, confused.

E–Frankie sat on the end of the bed. "I thought maybe we could have a kickabout?"

"It's night–time," said Frankie uneasily. "I've got school tomorrow." He paused. "You can't be here. People will find out."

E–Frankie looked glumly at the controller. "Oh," he said.

Frankie sat beside him. Across the room, in the mirror, he saw the two of them. *Like peas in a pod.* If he looked closely, he could see the differences, but he doubted anyone else could. And with that, an idea popped into his head.

Maybe my team don't have to pull out of the tournament after all. What if we've got the perfect substitute?

"I'll tell you what. Why don't you go back into the game for now, then come out tomorrow?"

E-Frankie's face lit up, his round eyes gleaming. "You promise?"

"Striker's honour," said Frankie. "In fact, I think you might be able to stay and have more than a kickaround. What about a real tournament?"

39

"I'd *love* that!" said E-Frankie. He pointed to the START button on the controller. "All you have to do is press that and I'll appear. Got it?"

"Got it," said Frankie, patting his new friend on the back.

E-Frankie jumped up. "See you later, mate!" he said. Then he pressed the EXIT button and the controller dropped to the carpet as he disappeared into thin air.

Frankie lay back on his bed, smiling to himself. The magic football had come to the rescue at exactly the right time!

CHAPTER 4

The first thing Frankie saw when he
woke up was the game controller
on his bedside table. He eyed the
START button and thought about
pressing It.

Not yet. Better to wait.

He couldn't wait to tell his
friends about his great idea.
He knew they'd be at the park
practising before school, so he

quickly dressed, had breakfast, and headed for the door with the controller in his pocket. Maybe it was his good mood, but his foot was feeling a bit better already.

"Not so fast!" said his dad. "Don't you want a lift?"

"It's okay," said Frankie, grabbing his crutches. "I can manage."

Max scampered up to the door with his lead in his mouth.

"Sorry, boy – I'm going to school straight after."

He hobbled to the park and saw Louise and Charlie over near the football goals. Because it was early

there was no one else about. As he
approached, they both waved.

"What are you grinning about?"
said Louise.

Frankie took out the controller.

"Thank goodness!" said Charlie.
"Is he back in the game?"

"For now," said Frankie. "But
listen — I've got a plan. What if
E-Frankie took my place on the
team?"

To Frankie's disappointment,
both his friends looked a bit unsure.

"What's the problem? No one
will know. And then you'll get to
play. Hannah and Kobi too!"

Slowly, a smile lit up Louise's

face, but still Charlie was frowning. "I guess so," he said at last. "He is sort of you, after all."

"Exactly!" said Frankie. He pressed the START button, and the air shimmered for a moment before his avatar appeared. E-Frankie grinned at Frankie and his friends.

Frankie explained his plan, and the game-boy nodded enthusiastically. "It would be a pleasure!" He pointed at the football. "Let's play!"

Charlie ran back to the goal, taking his position on the line. Frankie wished he could play too, but he remembered what the doctor had said. *If I don't let it get better, I could do more damage.*

Louise passed the ball to E-Frankie, who chipped it back into the air for her. Louise swung for a volley, but caught the ball slightly wrong and it spun off into the sky.

"Drat!" she said.

"Don't worry," said E-Frankie. "You just need to work on your hip turn. And keep your eye on the ball — forget about the goal. Let me show you."

Louise fetched the ball, then chipped it up for the avatar. With a perfect pivot, he sent the ball in an

arc over Charlie's outstretched hand
and into the goal.

Wow! thought Frankie, catching
Louise's eye. *That was some shot!*

Charlie didn't look all that
impressed, but then he hated it
when people managed to score
against him. He tossed the ball back
out, sulking.

"Have another try," said E-Frankie to Louise. "And remember, focus on the ball and getting power from your hips."

The next time, Louise hit the ball sweetly and ricocheted a shot at the goal. Charlie dived and just managed to save it at the near post.

"Great stop!" said E-Frankie.

Louise grinned at the avatar. "Great coaching!" she said.

They carried on for the next few minutes, going through drills. E-Frankie seemed only too happy to help, teaching Louise a new step-over technique, as well as how to curl the ball with the outside of her boot. Frankie wished he was playing too, but seeing his friends have fun was almost as good. Charlie even saved a few of the avatar's shots. They were having so much fun that they lost track of time. Frankie realised suddenly that it was almost nine o'clock.

"We've got to get to school in ten minutes!" he said. "Mr Donald will mark us late!"

"Can I come?" asked E-Frankie.

"Afraid not!" said Louise. "I don't think Donaldo would believe Frankie's suddenly got an identical twin."

"Ha!" said E-Frankie. "Never mind then. I guess it's bye for now. Same time tomorrow?"

"Sure," said Frankie. He pressed the EXIT button on the controller and the avatar vanished.

The three of them were late for school, because Frankie couldn't go as fast as normal. Kevin was lurking near the front door eating a bag of crisps.

"Where've you been?" he asked.

"Practising for the tournament," said Charlie.

"Why?" scoffed Kevin, spraying half-eaten crisps from his

mouth. "You haven't got a team, remember?"

Frankie shrugged. "Actually, my foot's feeling a bit better already," he said. "You'd better watch out next Saturday."

Kevin scowled. "We'll see, Frankenstein," he said.

"Inside, you lot!" called Mr Donald. Kevin scrunched the crisp packet and ran inside. Frankie followed more slowly. Mr Donald was standing with his arms folded crossly, but when he saw Frankie's leg he gasped.

"Oh dear, young man. Looks like you've come a cropper."

Frankie glanced at his friends and grinned. "Maybe," he said. "Maybe not."

As he came through the door, his crutches caught on the frame and he staggered. Almost in slow motion, he saw the game controller slide out of his pocket and clatter onto the floor.

Mr Donald didn't look impressed. "You know my rules about electronic devices at school, Frankie," he said. "I'm surprised at you."

"Sorry, sir," said Frankie.

Mr Donald stooped and picked it up. "Normally I'd confiscate it," he muttered, holding out the controller, "but as it's your first offence ..."

He must have pressed the START button, because behind him, E-Frankie blinked into life.

"Argh!" yelled Charlie.

"Whatever's wrong?" said Mr Donald.

The avatar was looking around, and opened his mouth, about to speak.

Frankie snatched the controller back and hit the EXIT button. E-Frankie vanished. *Phew!*

"Nothing, sir," said Charlie, white as a sheet. "Just thinking about maths later."

"Hmm. Off to your lessons," said Mr Donald.

Frankie's heart was still in his throat. He put the controller in his bag and zipped it up carefully. E-Frankie might be the perfect substitute, but if the secret got out ...

Well, it wasn't worth thinking about.

CHAPTER 5

The next two days passed
smoothly. Every morning at 8am,
Frankie met Louise and Charlie at
the empty park, and they practised
with Frankie's avatar. They met up
in the evening as well, and Frankie
lent his doppelganger a hoodie to
hide his face. Not that it would
have mattered if a stranger saw
them. It would just look like two

twin brothers playing with friends. Everyone was looking forward to the tournament on Saturday. With thirty-two teams altogether, it was a five-round knockout competition, with only one winner.

But as the week wore on, Frankie's avatar seemed to play better and better. He could do things with the ball that Frankie could only dream of – curling it metres left or right, or moving his feet so fast they were a blur. Once he did two hundred keepie-uppies, eyes closed, with just his left foot.

And as E-Frankie's skills got more impressive, his patience

seemed to get worse. If Louise
made a mistake, he would groan,
or sigh. On Wednesday afternoon,
after she hit the post, he actually
muttered something under his
breath that sounded like "Useless!"

"Pardon?" said Louise, red-faced.

"Nothing," said E-Frankie, with a
smile.

Frankie had heard it too, and it
troubled him. But every time they
pressed the EXIT button, E-Frankie
disappeared without complaining.

The good news was that his own
foot was getting better. He stopped
using the crutches on Wednesday, and
by Thursday afternoon when he went

for a check-up, he told the doctor he couldn't feel any discomfort at all.

"That's great news," said his mum.

"A full recovery!" said the doctor.

Frankie put his shoes back on. "So, does that mean I can play in the tournament on Saturday?"

"I don't see why not," said the doctor.

Frankie was so happy he could burst, until he realised what it meant.

I'll have to tell E-Frankie he's not playing.

He decided Friday morning would be the best time, when he met the others for practice. Charlie and Louise were both delighted he was better.

"To be honest," said Louise, "I was starting to find him a bit ..."

"Annoying?" said Charlie. "Patronising? Arrogant?"

Louise laughed. "Yeah, all of that. But, also, he's *very* good. It felt a bit like ... cheating."

"Okay," said Frankie, "but let's be nice. It'll be hard for him."

He took out the controller and pressed START.

E-Frankie appeared, already doing stretches. "What a great day! Can't wait to get started! Big tournament tomorrow!" He looked at Frankie and the others. "Why the long faces?"

"Um ... I'm sorry, but I've got some bad news," said Frankie. "We're really grateful for all your help, but my foot's recovered. We think it might be better if we just played the tournament as our original team."

The avatar's face fell. "Oh." But

then he smiled again. "I can still help you prepare though, right? One more game, for old times' sake?"

Frankie's heart flooded with relief. *He's taken it really well!*

"Of course!" he said.

Charlie took his place in the goal.

"Take it slow," said Louise, passing Frankie the ball. "You don't want to hurt yourself."

Frankie kicked the ball from foot to foot, feeling great. He'd really missed playing for the last week. He lined up at twenty yards out from goal, ready to shoot, then ...

"Watch out!" cried Louise.

Frankie saw his avatar skidding

in with both feet from just behind, and leapt into the air. E–Frankie slid beneath him, taking the ball.

Frankie stared at him, gobsmacked. "You could've broken my ankle with that challenge!" he said.

The avatar's lip curled in a sneer for a split second, but then became a smile. "Don't be silly – I was just messing around!"

Frankie still felt uneasy as they carried on playing. Maybe it had just been an accident, but it could easily have ended very badly. For a few minutes, they passed the ball between them more gently, sending shots at Charlie. He jumped around,

catching and deflecting with his gloves, then tossing the ball back to them.

We've got a great chance tomorrow, thought Frankie.

The ball landed in front of Louise. She backed up to take it on her chest, but suddenly E-Frankie was right there and shoulder-barged her over.

"Hey!" said Charlie. Frankie ran over towards his friend, but his avatar came right at him with the ball.

"Bet you can't tackle me," he said.

Louise was getting up already and Frankie was glad she was okay. Anger surged through Frankie's veins, and he stood square in front of his avatar. "That was out of order," he said.

E-Frankie laughed, and knocked the ball right between Frankie's legs. "Pathetic!" he called, as he dashed towards goal.

Charlie was ready, eyes focused on the ball as the avatar drew back his foot and blasted a shot like a cannonball. It hit Charlie right in the stomach, and he fell to the ground groaning. E-Frankie picked up the loose ball and side-footed it into the open goal. Lifting his arms, he roared, "Supergoal!"

Frankie went to Charlie's side. Their friend was wheezing still.

"You're horrible!" cried Louise, following on.

E–Frankie turned on them, his face raging. "And you lot are *losers*," he said. "You think you can just kick me out of the team, after everything I've done for you? You've not got a chance without me. I'm the best player the world has ever—"

He vanished before he could finish, and behind where he'd been standing Frankie saw Louise holding the controller, finger on the EXIT button.

"I've had quite enough of him!" she said.

CHAPTER 6

By the evening, Frankie's relief
had turned to guilt. His avatar had
behaved very badly, but perhaps it
was understandable. Frankie knew
how much he himself wanted to play
in the tournament — E-Frankie was
just disappointed and that's why
he'd reacted the way he did. Frankie
wondered if maybe he should
apologise. Just to clear the air.

He sat on his bed, and took the controller out of his bag. His thumb was hovering over the START button, when his brother came in without knocking. Frankie slid the controller under his pillow.

"My mate Jack saw you playing this morning in the park," said Kevin.

Frankie blushed. "Er . . . yeah — practising for the tournament."

"Who's the new friend?" asked Kevin. "Jack said he was pretty good. Running rings round you and Louise, blasting shots past Charlie . . ."

Frankie glanced up — his

brother's eyes were narrowed with suspicion.

"Oh, it's just ... Olly," said Frankie.

"Olly who?" said Kevin.

"I think he goes to St David's," said Frankie.

"If he's so good, I guess he's playing in the tournament? You can introduce me."

"Sure," said Frankie, licking his lips nervously.

"You're up to something," said Kevin.

"I don't know what you're talking about," Frankie replied. He just wanted to get Kevin out of his room. "Can you leave, please? Big day tomorrow!"

"Yeah," said Kevin, grinning unpleasantly. "You get to see my team lift the tournament trophy."

As his brother left, Frankie took out the controller again, but put it in his bedside drawer instead of pressing the START button. If Kevin was on to him, he didn't want to take any risks.

The following morning, Frankie felt a slight niggle in his foot again. Perhaps he'd overdone it slightly the day before. Still, he thought he could play. He went downstairs for breakfast, butterflies in his stomach. It was always the same before a big game. And what could be bigger than the town tournament?

Thankfully, Kevin seemed to have forgotten about their conversation the evening before, so there were no more awkward questions. *He's focused on the tournament too.*

After breakfast, Kevin set off to his friend Jack's house to meet the rest of his team. They were travelling to the football pitches together.

"See you later, Frankenstein," he said with a wave.

Frankie's mum and dad were looking forward to the tournament too. Mum was being a lineswoman, and Dad was due to help out with the barbecue afterwards.

"Meet you outside in ten minutes," said Mum. "We've got a few bits to load into the car."

Max barked. He thought he was going for a walk.

"Sorry, boy," said Frankie's dad. "You're not allowed — you weed on the goalposts last time, remember?"

Max trotted back into the kitchen and flopped down in his basket.

Frankie went upstairs to get dressed in his tracksuit, and pack his kitbag.

He was about to leave his room when his eyes fell on the bedside drawer. He wondered what E-Frankie was doing at the moment. Was he sad, or angry? Did he feel anything at all when he was in the game?

Frankie looked out of his bedroom door and saw his mum and dad carrying bags of burger buns and drinks to the front door. *They'll be busy for a couple of minutes.* So he took out the controller and pressed the START button.

E-Frankie appeared in the middle of his room. When he saw Frankie, he looked down at his feet, ashamed.

"I'm sorry," he mumbled. "I wasn't very nice."

Frankie was glad to see his avatar wasn't angry anymore. "It's okay," he replied. "I know how much you were looking forward to the tournament. It just didn't seem right. Y'know – you're so good at football, you could probably win single-handed."

"Single-footed, more like!" said E-Frankie, with a shy smile.

Frankie laughed. "I want to thank you though – you helped us so much this week."

"No problem," said E-Frankie. "How are you feeling? Foot all right?"

"Just about," said Frankie.

From downstairs, the car horn beeped. Mum and Dad were ready.

"I've got to go," said Frankie. He

pointed to his kitbag. "Stuff's all ready."

E–Frankie leant down and picked up the bag, holding it out to Frankie. "Good luck!" he said.

As Frankie reached for it, his avatar snatched the controller from his hand.

"Hey! What are you—"

A hand shoved him in the chest and sent him staggering backwards. He tripped, falling into his wardrobe. Then the door slammed. Frankie scrambled to his feet and tried to open it, but something blocked the door from the other side.

"Let me out!" he cried.

The car horn honked again, the sound muffled slightly among the hanging clothes.

"I'm coming!" called E-Frankie.

In the darkness, Frankie banged his fists against the doors. "Help me!" he called. "Mum! Dad!"

But all he heard was the sound of his avatar's feet pounding down the stairs, then the front door slamming shut.

I'm trapped!

CHAPTER 7

Frankie thrust his shoulder at the door several times, but he couldn't get the wardrobe open. *How could I have been so stupid? I should never have let him out again!*

He slid down to the ground in despair. There was nothing he could do. E-Frankie was obviously planning to take his place, but what about afterwards? How could he explain to his mum and dad that he had locked himself in a wardrobe? Fumbling in the dark, his hands found the scuffed leather of the magic football.

"You got us into his mess!" he said angrily.

But even as he said those words, he knew it wasn't exactly true. The football had brought out the avatar the first time, but it was Frankie who'd pressed the START button on the controller every morning. He'd been ready to use E-Frankie as a substitute — it had seemed so straightforward.

But there are no shortcuts to winning, he thought.

It was hard to tell how much time passed. He wondered if the tournament had started and how the teams were getting on. Kobi and Hannah probably wouldn't be able to tell it wasn't really him on their team, but maybe Louise and Charlie would notice ...

Something growled on the other side of the door. "Who's in there?" barked a voice.

"Max!" cried Frankie. "Max – it's me!"

"Frankie?"

"He locked me in! The avatar!"

"I can see that," said Max. "He's jammed the handle with a chair ..."

Frankie heard a crash, then tried the handle again and the door opened. Max was wagging his tail next to the fallen chair.

"Thanks, boy!" Frankie said.

He looked at his bedside alarm clock. It was already 11:30. The tournament had started an hour

before. Perhaps if he dashed there, there'd be time to do something about E-Frankie. He had no idea what though.

"Let's go," he said to Max, dashing to the front door.

"I thought I wasn't allowed," said Max. "Your dad said . . ."

"Never mind that!" said Frankie. "We've got a rogue avatar to catch!"

Frankie ran all the way to the football pitches on the edge of town, with Max trotting along on the lead. His dog was panting by the time they got there, and Frankie was soaked with sweat. There were several teams in different strips milling around, and the smell of barbecuing meat filled the air. Frankie's heart sank.

We're too late. It's over.

But where was E-Frankie?

"Hey! Good work today!" called a voice. Frankie turned and saw Mr Donald holding some sort of bun in a napkin, waving to him. "Your dad makes a great hot dog!"

Frankie waved back. He realised he needed to be careful. He had to find E-Frankie, but they couldn't be seen together.

He led Max towards the changing block. "Let's separate," he said. "Try

to sniff him out but don't let Mum
or Dad see you."

"Got it," said Max, running off.

Frankie met Louise coming
through a door, still in her kit. She
grinned widely. "We were just
wondering where you'd got to!" she
said. "You're changed already! It's
the trophy ceremony any minute."

"Louise, he's *here!*" said Frankie.

She frowned. "Who?"

"E-Frankie!"

Charlie came jogging up, and
grabbed Frankie's arm. "There you
are! Come on!"

Frankie didn't get the chance
to say anything else to Charlie

or Louise because they were walking through crowds of people and players towards a makeshift podium near the centre of one of the pitches. A silver cup sat on the top. Hannah and Kobi were there too, standing beside the town mayor, Dr Fisher, wearing her official chains. Frankie's teammates smiled at him, and all the spectators were staring his way, clapping.

The mayor waited for quiet.

"What a tournament it's been," she said. "So many examples of teamwork, sportsmanship and talent. Everyone who took part deserves a round of applause, but there can only be one winning team." She picked up the trophy. "It's my great pleasure to present this year's five-a-side trophy to the captain of our worthy victors!"

She extended the trophy to Frankie, who just stared at it. *This isn't right at all. I can't take it.*

Everyone was watching, and Kobi muttered under his breath. "Frankie, what's up?"

But Frankie was looking out at the crowd, searching for his own face. *Is he here still?* He saw his mum and dad, beaming proudly — Charlie and Louise's parents too.

And there was his brother Kevin, wearing his usual scowl.

Eventually, Charlie grabbed the trophy and lifted it into the air. The crowd broke into wild applause and cheering. As it died down, Frankie saw Louise whispering to Charlie, and his friend's face went pale.

"We need to talk," said Frankie. "Let's find somewhere quiet."

They left Kobi and Hannah celebrating with the trophy, and went back to the changing room where Max was waiting. "No sign," he said. "He doesn't have a scent though. Probably because he's not real."

"He was real enough to play in

the tournament," said Frankie, as they went inside. There was no one else in the changing room.

"What?" gasped Charlie. "That wasn't really you playing?"

Frankie shook his head. "Wasn't it obvious?"

Louise groaned. "He must have messed up his hair. He's cleverer than we thought. He didn't even play that well sometimes. He made mistakes. We thought it was because you weren't 100% fit."

"But you still won the whole tournament?" said Frankie. He felt sick.

Louise explained quickly what

had happened over the five games, how they'd been close to losing a few times, only for the team to pull together and scrape through.

"It was Kevin's team and us in the final," said Charlie. "You ... I mean, the other you, he scored the winning goal. It was amazing — an overheard kick. Almost unbelievable."

"I bet it was," said Frankie sadly.

"So, what do we do now?" asked Louise.

A figure stepped out from behind a curtain of hanging coats. It was Kevin and he looked furious.

"You could start by telling me exactly what's going on," he said.

CHAPTER 8

It was no use hiding the truth from Frankie's brother now. It wasn't really fair to, either.

"This is something to do with the magic football, isn't it?" said Kevin.

Frankie nodded, and began to explain, starting with the evening they'd played *FantasyScorer2* in his brother's room. Kevin listened patiently, looking sometimes amazed, sometimes almost smiling, but mainly cross.

". . . and then he locked me in my wardrobe," Frankie said. "That's about it."

"No, it's not," said Kevin. "You missed the part where he took your place in the tournament and cheated my team out of the trophy. I've a good mind to go out there right now and tell the mayor and all those spectators *exactly* what happened!"

"No!" said Charlie and Louise together.

"Why shouldn't I?" said Kevin. "You're always lecturing me about fair play and honesty. The boot's on the other foot now, though, isn't it?"

"Please," said Frankie. "It was a mistake. We're sorry."

"*Sorry* won't give me the trophy," said Kevin.

"There's no saying you would have won anyway," protested Charlie.

Frankie glared at his friend. *Don't wind him up!*

"Tell you what," said Frankie. "If you keep quiet, I'll do the dishes — for a month!"

Kevin scoffed. "Two months."

"Done," said Frankie.

"And clean my room," said Kevin.

Frankie thought about his brother's disgusting bedroom and flinched. *I've got no choice. If Kev tells everyone about the magic football, they'll take it away.*

"All right," he said.

Kevin grinned and rubbed his hands together. "Cool. Let's find this little cheat then, shall we?"

"You're going to help?" said Louise.

"Course I am. He made a fool of me on the pitch. Time for some payback."

Max scampered in. "Frankie – your mum and dad are coming!" he barked.

"Hide!" said Frankie.

"Where?" said Max.

Frankie glanced around, then saw the bin full of used football kit. He picked Max up and dropped him in. His dog burrowed down, and his tail had just vanished as Frankie's mum put her head around the door. "Come on, Kev, time to— Oh! Frankie?"

"Hi, Mum," he said, trying to look calm.

"I thought you said you were going home?"

"Did I?"

His mum wore a puzzled smile. "Yes, ten minutes ago. You asked for a key. I watched you go."

97

Frankie's blood ran cold. *The avatar . . .*

"Just realised I'd forgotten my kit bag!" said Frankie.

"Well, listen, Dad and I are going to stay and help with the clear-up, so we'll see you back at home later." His mum turned to go, then looked back. "That was the best goal you've ever scored," she said. "We're so proud of you."

After she'd gone, Kevin looked back at them with his eyebrows raised. "The best goal you've ever scored!" he repeated, in a squeaky voice. "Oh, *please*!"

"Why's he heading back to your

house?" said Louise. "Surely he knows we'll find him there."

"It might have been a lie," said Charlie, stroking his chin with his goalie glove.

"Or ... there's something he wants there," said Frankie, and he shuddered when he realised what it could be.

"My comics?" said Kevin.

Frankie shook his head. "Worse. The magic football!"

The front door was open, and they paused outside. "If you see him, grab him," said Frankie. "But the most important thing is the controller. We can send him back if we hit the EXIT button."

As soon as Frankie was inside, he saw muddy footprints on the stairs. Max growled. Frankie led the way, treading slowly. The footprints led into his bedroom. "Hello?" he called, but there was no answer.

Frankie edged into his room, expecting to see E-Frankie within. But on the floor was a pair of dirty football boots. The chair was still lying on its side and the wardrobe door hung open. Frankie dashed over to it, and his fears were confirmed. The football was gone, and there was no sign of his avatar.

"Where is he?" said Louise.

"Hey, guys!" called Kevin from next door. "I've found something."

Frankie and his friends dashed into Kevin's room. The game controller lay on the carpet by Kevin's foot. Frankie's brother was pointing at his TV. There was a loading screen for FantasyScorer2.

"How is that possible?" said Charlie. "The game isn't even connected."

The loading screen disappeared and was replaced by the character set-up one. There stood E-Frankie, hands behind his back.

"Hi there, team!" he said.

101

Frankie moved closer, reaching out and touching the screen with his fingertips. "You're back in the game," he said.

"Correct," said E-Frankie. "Only now I have this!"

He took his hands from behind his back to reveal the magic

football. With a flick, he spun it on his finger.

"Thief!" said Louise.

"Liar!" said Charlie.

"Cheat!" said Kevin.

"I prefer 'winner'," said the avatar.

Frankie picked up the controller and hit the START button, but nothing happened.

"Nice try," said his double, "but now I've got this, the game's under my control."

Frankie glanced at his friends. "What can we do?"

"I say we switch him off once and for all," said Kevin.

"But then we lose the football," said Louise. "And there's no saying what he can do with it. He might be able to escape again."

Frankie tried to ignore his avatar's smug face. *I should have seen from the start what he is. All he cares about is winning at any cost.*

And that gave him an idea. A mad one, but it was worth a try.

"You know, you're good," he said. "But you're just a computer program."

E–Frankie's face flushed red. "*Just.* Computers beat real people easily."

"Prove it," said Frankie. "Unless you're scared."

"I'm not scared of anyone," spat the avatar.

It's working — I'm getting to him.

"Then come out," Frankie said. "Face me one on one."

Frankie sensed his friends staring intently. *Do they realise I'm trying to trick him?*

E-Frankie dropped the ball at his feet. "I've got a better idea. Why don't we have a proper match? My team versus yours?"

"Your team?" said Louise. "I'm not sure we want a bunch of crazy avatars running around our town."

E–Frankie's lips twisted in a mischievous smirk. "Who said anything about your town?"

He drew back his foot and kicked the ball straight at them. It burst through the screen, and Frankie threw up his hands, expecting a shower of broken glass. But instead the walls of the bedroom seemed to blur into interlocking blocks of colour. He heard Louise gasp and looked at his friend. She was flickering in and out of existence.

"What's happening?" said Charlie. He was staring at his gloves. They looked oddly blocky

too, as if they were turning into pixels.

Then the room vanished, and Frankie was staring up at stands of football terraces on every side. Thousands of motionless faces looked back. He glanced down and saw grass under his feet. The air tasted stale. His friends, his brother and Max were standing right as they had been in Kevin's room.

But we're a long way from Kevin's room now . . .

CHAPTER 9

The magic football rolled to Frankie's feet, and he saw his avatar standing a few metres away.

"Welcome to *my* world," he said.

"We're in the game," said Kevin, turning on the spot. "How do we get out?"

"You don't," said E-Frankie. "Unless you can beat us."

"Who's *us*?" said Frankie. "I only see you."

E–Frankie clicked his fingers, and from a tunnel several players emerged. He rubbed his eyes. They looked just like his friends. First came a version of Louise, with a long dark ponytail. Next came a freckled redhead with goalie gloves who ran to stand between two posts. After him, a little dog that bore more than a passing resemblance to Max. The only one who didn't really match was the last, a tall, muscle–bound player with a shaved head.

"They're our avatars," said Louise.

"Correct," said E-Frankie. "You designed us. And now we're going to teach you a footballing lesson you'll never forget."

Frankie looked at the magic football, then at his friends. They'd already played a five-match tournament today. They were tired. He could feel his own foot throbbing slightly. But he knew it was the only chance they had.

"Let's play," he said.

E-Frankie pointed to a giant display above the side of the ground and a clock flashed up *5:00.*

Five minutes to save our skins . . .

A whistle went, and E-Frankie
ran at the ball.

Game on . . .

Frankie passed to Louise, as
Charlie sprinted back towards
the goal. Louise passed to Kevin.
But Louise's avatar was charging
at him, and then something very
strange indeed happened. In the
blink of an eye, there were two of
her, splitting off from one another.
Kevin panicked and tried to kick the
ball to Max, but one of the Louises
intercepted it, then passed to the
other.

Now they've got six players!

Max tried to tackle the one with

the ball, but she passed to the
other.

"Take one each!" Frankie called
to the real Louise. They both ran to
intercept, only for the ball to loop
across to E-Frankie. He blasted
a shot towards the top corner so
fast Frankie's eyes could barely

follow it. But the net didn't balloon, and Frankie saw that Charlie had somehow managed to catch it.

"You cheated!" said Louise.

The twin Louise avatars merged back into one again. "We all have special skills," she said.

Charlie rolled the ball out to Max. Straight away E-Frankie was sprinting towards him with superhuman speed. But Max was ready and kicked a perfect pass to Kevin. This time, as E-Louise split, Kevin ran right between them. Frankie called for the pass, and just as Kev looked up, the ground in front of him burst open. The avatar

dog emerged, his jaws gnashing
with earth, and Kevin tripped over.
E-Louise picked up the loose ball,
and passed to E-Frankie. Again, his
burst of speed took him past first
Louise, then Frankie. This time, as
he ran at goal, he shouted, "Stop
this if you can!" and as the ball
left his foot it burst into flames.
Charlie ducked and it slammed into
the net.

"You can't do that!" said Charlie.

"Our pitch, our rules," said
E-Frankie.

Frankie grabbed the smoking
ball, and carried it back to the
centre circle. "We've played

cheats before," he said to Louise, who was looking grim. "We just need to keep our cool. Use your dribbling to draw them in, then pass to me."

The whistle went and they kicked off. Louise took the ball down the wing, skipping around her two copies. E-Frankie was already running towards goal, obviously expecting the ball any moment. Frankie couldn't see E-Max at all, but then the ground in front of Louise began to shift.

"Now!" he called.

Louise released the perfect looping pass right to his feet just as the dog tunnelled out of the pitch. Now it was just the hulking E-Kev between him and goal.

But the massive defender wasn't even moving at all. *Maybe this will be easier than I thought.* He was about to shoot when E-Kev simply stamped his foot. The ground shook like an earthquake and Frankie fell flat on his backside. The ball rolled to a halt in front of the opposition keeper, Charlie's avatar. As he picked it up, his hands seemed to balloon to the size of dinner platters. *More cheating!* He hurled the ball with astonishing power, right the way up-field to E-Frankie. Another fireball streaked past Charlie. He managed bravely to get his hand to it, but all he managed to do was deflect it into the goal and set his glove on fire. He shook the glove off and stamped out the flames. "I'm sorry," he said. "I don't know what to do."

Frankie picked himself up. He felt dreadful for his friend.

The clock read 3:51.

Just over a minute gone, and we're already 2–0 down!

As Frankie headed back for the restart, he saw that Kevin's head was hanging low, as was Max's tail.

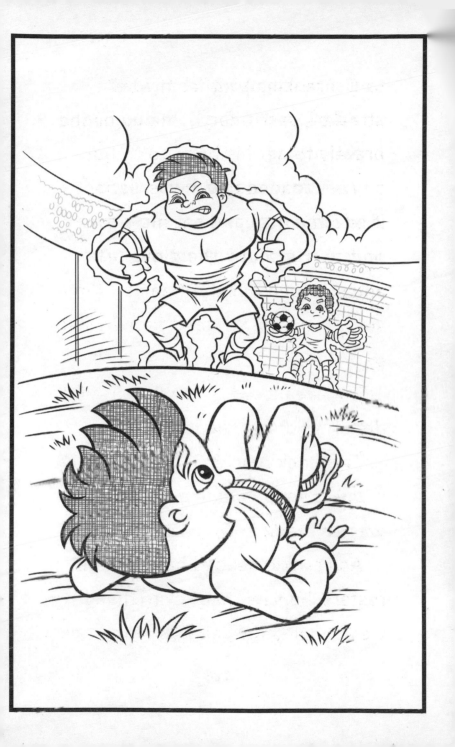

Louise was limping from where she'd tripped in the hole dug by the cheating dog.

They're giving up, he realised. *And I'm not surprised. There's no way we can win against this team.*

CHAPTER 10

Frankie was placing the ball in the centre circle when a movement in the tunnel caught his eye. It was a man in a black strip, ropes pinning his arms to his side, and more tying his ankles.

"That looks like a referee!" he said to Louise.

She glanced over, too, and her eyes widened. "Don't you

remember?" she said. "When Kevin was playing the game, he put on some sort of cheat mode and the icon showed the ref tied up. I bet that's how they're winning."

"So, if we free the ref, we level the playing field," said Frankie. He whistled to Max.

"Get a move on," said E-Frankie. "It's your time you're wasting — 2:58 on the clock!"

Frankie whispered to Max. "You need to free the ref," he said, and nodded in the direction of the tunnel.

"Got it!" said his dog.

Frankie kicked off, but instead

of running forward, he went back.
He needed to draw the other team
as far from the tunnel as possible.
Confused, E-Max and Frankie's
avatar followed. The real Max ran
in the other direction. But as they
closed in, Frankie passed the ball to
Charlie.

"You're shooting the wrong way,"
laughed E-Frankie. "Two minutes
thirty left."

Max had disappeared into the
tunnel. *Come on, boy, you can do it!*

Charlie kicked the ball long to
Louise. Her twin avatars closed in,
but she passed to Kevin. He still had
to manoeuvre past the giant though,

and after that, the huge-handed keeper waited, ready to stop any shot.

E-Kev stamped his foot once more, but this time nothing happened.

"Huh?" he said. Kevin continued on goal.

The avatar keeper spread his arms, and as he did, his hands shrank to normal size. Kevin took a shot, and buried the ball in the bottom corner. As he lifted his arms, Frankie and his teammates cheered.

"What happened?" E-Frankie scowled.

E-Louise pointed at the tunnel, where the ref was emerging, trailing gnawed-through ropes. Max ran past him, tail wagging.

"Now let's see who's best," said Frankie.

His avatar looked ready to explode as he took his place in the

centre circle. "We're still faster and stronger than you," he said. "You designed us, remember?"

"That might be true," said Louise, "but we've played together all our lives."

"We're a *team*," added Charlie.

The ref blew the whistle, and E-Frankie passed to his dog, who headed the ball to Louise's avatar. Louise met her in a hard tackle, and managed to get the ball. Kevin's giant avatar blocked her path. With nowhere to go, Louise tried to pass to Max, but E-Frankie slipped in like a blur and took the ball. *Even without the cheats he's quicker than any of us,* thought Frankie. He ran after his avatar, and tried to tackle. E-Frankie skipped past. Next Kevin tried and failed. Charlie ran out of goal to stop the run, but E-Frankie did a series of rapid step-overs, leaving Charlie sprawling. He stopped a metre from the goal-line, foot on the ball.

"Looks like we're going 3-1 up," he said.

As he was about to kick the ball in, Max darted across the pitch quicker than if he was chasing a squirrel in the park. He head-butted the ball from under E-Frankie's boot, then dribbled it up the pitch.

He passed to Kev, who took one touch and passed to Louise. She danced around the dog, then E-Kev, before crashing a shot towards goal. The keeper stood no chance, and suddenly it was two-all.

"Go, Lou!" shouted Frankie.

E-Frankie was red-faced.

"It doesn't matter," he said, nodding at the clock, which read 00.48. "You'll never score in time to get out."

As the game kicked off again, E-Frankie passed the ball to Louise's avatar. She passed it back to E-Max, who squared it to the giant Kev.

The seconds were ticking down, and as they did Frankie's heart rose into his throat. *They're wasting time.*

He ordered his team up-field to crowd the ball, and E-Kev panicked, mistiming a pass. Frankie latched on and dribbled towards goal. Above his head, he saw they were down to the last ten seconds. *I'll only get one chance.*

The goalkeeper spread his arms. From the corner of his right eye, Frankie saw E-Lou rushing in, so he went left, then readied his shot. He was about to shoot when E-Frankie slid in for a tackle. Searing agony shot up Frankie's ankle and he rolled across the ground clutching his foot.

Somewhere a whistle went, but he barely heard it. Tears threatened to squeeze from his eyes.

"Oops," said E-Frankie. Frankie saw his avatar standing over him, doing a terrible job of looking concerned.

Frankie's teammates rushed to his side, as waves of pain rose from his foot.

"You did it on purpose," he said. "You knew that was my injured foot."

The ref blew the whistle again, and pointed to the penalty spot.

The clock had stopped at four seconds.

Frankie picked himself up. As he tried to put weight on his ankle, he had to grit his teeth against the pain.

"Want me to take it?" said Louise. But Frankie could see she looked nervous.

"I'll do it," said Kevin.

"It's okay," said Frankie. *I'll show them.*

He placed the ball on the penalty spot, and all of the avatar team crowded closer. "Last kick of the match," said E-Frankie.

"You've got no chance," said E-Louise.

"Game over," said E-Charlie on the goal-line.

Frankie blocked them all out, and hobbled backwards. He'd won one tournament unfairly today. Time to make up for that.

He stared at the magic football. Normally it sent them to help people, or solve problems, but this time it had set him a test.

And I intend to pass.

The ref blew and with three strides, Frankie reached the ball and fired it towards the goal. From the moment it left his boot, he knew it was good. He saw E-Charlie dive, but the ball ricocheted off the inside of the post and into the net. At the same time the clock hit 00:00.

"Nooooo!" screamed E-Frankie, falling to his knees. Frankie felt hands lifting him into the air as his friends and his brother hoisted him up. Max spun in excited circles at their feet.

All around the stadium, the spectators rose and clapped. He closed his eyes and soaked it all in . . .

"What on earth are you doing?" said his dad's voice.

Frankie opened his eyes and saw the pitch had gone and they were back in Kevin's bedroom. His head was dangerously close to the light-shade. He felt a bit dizzy. His dad frowned. "It's just a computer game, you know?"

Frankie saw the TV screen was showing a banner saying "YOU WIN!"

His friends lowered him to the ground gently. Max had the magic football under his paws.

"Sometimes you get quite into it," said Charlie.

"Okay, fine," said Frankie's dad. "But maybe ease off on the celebrations before you come through the ceiling. And Kevin – this room looks like a bombsite. Clean it up."

He ducked away again. After
a few seconds, Frankie and his
friends burst out laughing.

Louise had picked up the
controller. She pressed a button,
and the screen displayed a tab:
WOULD YOU LIKE TO PLAY
AGAIN?

Charlie jumped across the room,
and switched off the TV. "Definitely
not, thank you!"

"I agree," said Louise. "I've had
quite enough computer games for a
while."

Frankie gingerly tested his ankle.
Oddly, the pain had gone.

Max nosed the football towards

Frankie. "Looks like someone wants a *real* game," said Frankie.

"Let's go to the park!" said Louise.

As they all bundled out of the room, Kevin called out, "Um ... have you forgotten something, Frankenstein?" He waved a hand towards the mess in his room. "We had a deal, remember?"

Frankie groaned. "I'll catch you guys up," he said.

But instead of leaving, Charlie and Louise turned around and came back in.

"We'll get it done quicker if we all help," said Lou.

Charlie picked up a pair of underpants, holding them at arm's length. "Yeah, I guess so."

Frankie smiled. He could always rely on his teammates.

ACKNOWLEDGEMENTS

Many thanks to everyone at Hachette Children's Group; Neil Blair, Zoe King, Daniel Teweles and all at The Blair Partnership; Kieron Ward for bringing my characters to life; special thanks to Michael Ford for all his wisdom and patience; and to Steve Kutner for being a great friend and for all his help and guidance, not just with the book but with everything.

Frankie and his friends have
been on so many adventures,
taking them all over the world!

Turn the page for an
extract from another one of
Frank Lampard's books:
Meteor Madness ...

Frankie and his friends are staying at a holiday camp which is supposed to have its own theme park. Unfortunately, the theme park is closed, but it's the perfect place for the magic football to send them on an adventure — read on to find out what happens!

Frankie cast a nervous glance back as he pushed through the gate of the empty theme park. Everything was still, apart from some coloured lights flashing further into the park. Frankie's skin tingled. Had the power come back on? Or was this the work of the magic football? It wouldn't be the first time it had made strange things happen.

Most of the rides were silent. He saw a roller coaster, a clown's circus, a ghost house and several others. The flashing lights were coming from a model space shuttle supported by a long beam. Frankie guessed it swung up and down. The ride was called "Galaxy Quest".

But he couldn't see the ball anywhere.

Max trotted up to the spaceship and sniffed around. Then he rested his paws on it.

"I think he's smelled something," said Frankie. Leaning over the spaceship's edge, he saw the ball lodged under one of the seats. "It's here!" Frankie jumped up into the ride.

"Cool!" said Charlie, climbing up

as well. "I've always wanted to be an astronaut! One small save for man, one giant save for—"

He went quiet as the ride creaked into motion, swinging slowly forwards on the long arm. Frankie stumbled backwards on to one of the seats.

"Er . . . is it supposed to do that?" said Louise. "Maybe I should go and get someone."

The ride rocked backwards again. Frankie saw the ball was glowing a little.

"I think it's the magic of the football," he said. "It must want us to go. Quick, climb in!"

Louise grabbed Max and passed him to Frankie as the spaceship swung back and forth. Then she scrambled in herself. "Fasten your seatbelts!" she cried.

The ride moved faster, swinging high into the air. Frankie's stomach yo-yoed up and down, but he pulled down the harness bars over his head until they clicked into place. He held Max in his lap.

"Do you think it's safe?" Charlie shouted.

"I trust the football!" said Frankie, as the shuttle rocked higher.

The spaceship swooped downwards, then climbed up the

other side. This time it didn't stop and swung upside-down, before plummeting again. "It's getting faster!" shouted Louise.

The forest and the other rides shot past as the spaceship dipped and rose in huge circles. Frankie wondered if he'd made a mistake. What if the ride was actually dangerous?

He saw smoke coming from the arm that held the rocket.

"We should get off!" cried Charlie.

Sparks fizzed in all directions. Then, with a few pops, the bolts and screws exploded. The whole ride began to shake. "It's falling to bits!" yelled Loulse.

Max was trembling on Frankie's knee, and he held him tight. They spun faster and faster, until everything was a blur.

Then as the rocket rose again, Frankie felt it lurch. With a horrible tear of metal, they shot into the sky.

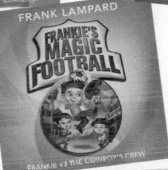

FRANKIE'S MAGIC FOOTBALL WEBSITE

Have you had a chance to check out **frankiesmagicfootball.co.uk** yet?

Get involved in **competitions**, find out **news** and **updates** about the series, play **games** and watch **videos** featuring the author, **Frank Lampard!**

Visit the site to join **Frankie's FC** today!